Inside, Inside, Inside

Written and Illustrated by Holly Meade

Marshall Cavendish
New York London Singapore

Hey, Noah, I found your blue crystal pee wee marble under my bed.

I wondered where that went.
Thanks, Jenny.

Where should I put it?
How about inside this salt shaker?
OK. What about the salt?
I'll make a pile.

Now what are you doing?
Closing the salt shaker
inside this cereal box.
What for, Noah?
For fun.
What about the cereal?
I'll eat it later.

The cereal box will just fit inside this recipe box.
Noah, won't Mom get mad?
Mad?

You know, about the salt
and the cereal?
Well...she's not up yet.

Do we put the recipe box
inside another box?
Hmmmm . . . we don't have
another box.

We have this hat.
WE?!
That's MY hat.
Well, then, we have
your hat.

A book
that is
shut but
is but
a block
PROVER

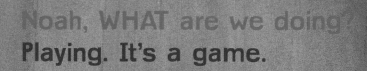

Noah, WHAT are we doing?
Playing. It's a game.

What game?
Inside, Inside, Inside.
Inside, Inside, Inside?
Yup. In goes your hat!

OK, I want to play.
How about my pillowcase?
Perfect, Jenny.

Do we just leave the
pillow on the floor?
Sure, for now.

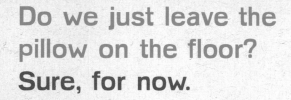

What do you think, should we try
Dad's jacket next?
We could zipper it all inside.

Yeah, but won't Dad need his jacket today?
Hmmmm...maybe.

Let's see if we can get the jacket
inside the hamper.
Pee-yew! Smelly clothes.

Perfect fit!
Is that the end of the game?
No. Help me carry it to the shower.

THAT'S the end of the game.
How come, Noah?
Because we can't put the shower
inside anything. It's already inside
the bathroom.

And the bathroom's inside the house.
And the house is inside . . . Noah,
what's the house inside of?
Inside the neighborhood, I guess.
That was fun. Want to play again?
No, let's draw instead.
Draw what?

An Inside, Inside, Inside picture.
OK.
I'm going to start with the shower.
I'm good at drawing moons.
That's good. We'll need a moon.

I broke a crayon.
That's OK.
I'm going to draw what's OUTSIDE the insides!
OK, Noah?

OK. I've drawn the shower, house, neighborhood,
town, state, and next is the country. I'm not
sure of the shape. I'd better get a book!

This takes a long time,
doesn't it, Noah?
Yeah, but it's worth it.
Why?

**Because it is. Mom says
art's worth it.**

Is this art?

Yup.

I'm going to try Saturn. It has
hula hoops around it.

Rings, Jenny.

Right, rings.

**What we're drawing on the edges
is called the solar system.**

Oh.

We did it, Noah!
Can you remember where
we started?
The shower?
No, REALLY started.

Oh! We started with your blue crystal pee wee marble.
Yup, and then?
You put the marble inside the salt shaker, and the salt shaker went inside the cereal box. Then came the recipe box, which went inside the . . . what did the recipe box go inside of?

Your hat!
Oh, yeah, my hat.
Do you think my hat is all right?
Probably. Then what?
Noah, I really like my hat.
Maybe we should check on it.
My crystal pee wee is my favorite marble,
and I'm not worried about it.
Hmmmm . . . I guess . . . OK.
My hat went inside the wastebasket,
which went inside the pillowcase,
which went inside Dad's jacket,
which . . . ummmm . . . went inside the
hamper. And we put that inside the shower!
Good job, Jenny!
Thanks.

I'll say the rest.
The shower's inside the bathroom,
inside the house,
inside the neighborhood,
inside the town,
inside the state,
inside the country,
inside the continent,
inside the world,
inside the solar system,
Inside, Inside, Inside!

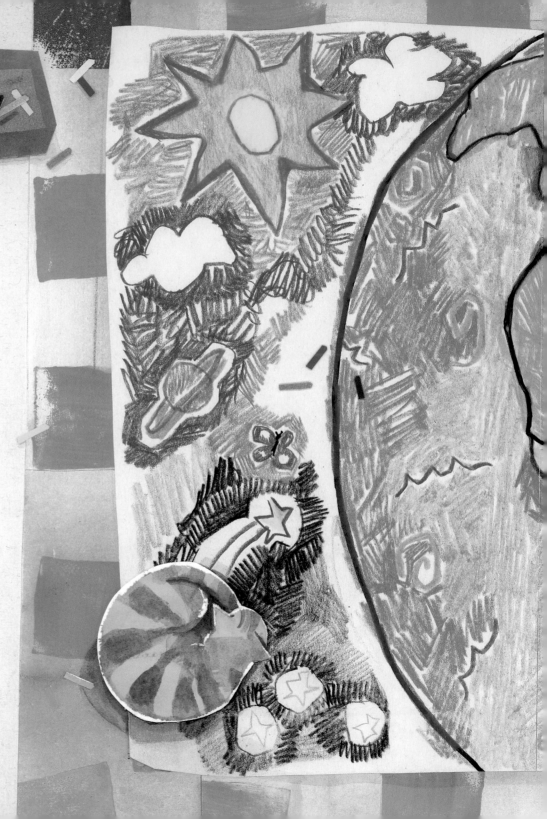

What's the solar system inside of?
The Milky Way galaxy. But we'd need
a much bigger piece of paper.
What's the Milky Way galaxy inside of?
Hmmmm . . . I don't know, Jenny.
Let's get a snack.

Hey! Cookies go
inside of me!
Yeah, but let's play
something else now.

NOAH!!!

NOAH!!! JENNY!!!

For Jenny Nicole and Noah Meade, with all my love —H. M.

Text and illustrations copyright © 2005 by Holly Meade
All rights reserved
Marshall Cavendish, 99 White Plains Road, Tarrytown, NY 10591
www.marshallcavendish.us
Library of Congress Cataloging-in-Publication Data

Meade, Holly.
Inside, inside, inside / written and illustrated by Holly Meade.
p. cm.
Summary: Noah and Jenny play a game in which they place one item inside another, over and over, until they place it all in the shower,
then imagine and draw the shower inside the house, inside the neighborhood, and all the way to the solar system.
ISBN 0-7614-5125-0
[1. Games--Fiction. 2. Brothers and sisters—Fiction. I.] I. Title.

PZ7.M4795In 2005
[E]—dc22
2004019321

The text of this book is set in Imperfect Bold.
The collage illustrations are rendered in cut paper and watercolor.

Printed in China
First edition
1 2 4 6 5 3